Charlotte the Sunflower Fairy

by Daisy Meadows

ORCHARD BOOKS

www.rainbowmagic.co.uk

The Fairyland Palace
Blossom Hall
Fairy Garden
Leafley Village
Visitors' Centre

Jack Frost's
Ice Castle
ssom Lake
Picnic Spot
The Park
Petal Perfection
Flower Shop
Blossom Village
High St
Rainbow Falls Gardens
Chaney Court Flower Show

I need the magic petals' powers,
To give my castle garden flowers.
And so I use my magic well
To work against the fairies' spell.

From my wand ice magic flies,
Frosty bolt through fairy skies.
And this crafty spell I weave
To bring the petals back to me.

Contents

Village Visit

"'Welcome to Leafley'," Rachel Walker read out as she and her best friend Kirsty Tate stopped at the noticeboard outside the pretty Visitors' Centre. "'Come and see our beautiful village and our early-blooming sunflowers!'"

"Isn't Leafley a brilliant name for a village?" Kirsty laughed, as she and

Rachel waited for their parents to catch them up. The Tates and the Walkers, along with Rachel's dog, Buttons, were spending the Easter holidays together at nearby Blossom Hall hotel. "You kind of expect a place called Leafley to be full of beautiful flowers."

Rachel nodded, and then looked serious. "But will the Leafley sunflowers be blooming at all, now that the Petal Fairies' magic petals are missing?" she asked anxiously.

Kirsty frowned. "Good question. We haven't found Charlotte the Sunflower Fairy's petal yet!" she exclaimed.

At the beginning of their holiday the two girls had promised to help their fairy friends find the seven magic petals. The petals were very important because their magic made sure that all the flowers in the human world bloomed beautifully. Cold, crafty Jack Frost had wanted the magic petals to make flowers grow in the frozen grounds around his ice castle, and so he'd sent his naughty goblin servants to steal them and bring them to him. But in a battle of spells between Jack Frost and the fairies, the petals had spun away into the human world in a whirl of pink and white magic. Now

Rachel and Kirsty and the Petal Fairies were trying to return all the petals to Fairyland before the goblins got hold of them again.

"We've already helped Tia the Tulip Fairy, Louise the Lily Fairy and Pippa the Poppy Fairy," said Kirsty. "Maybe we'll find another petal today."

"I hope so," Rachel agreed, as their parents joined them.

"Come on, girls," said Mrs Walker, ushering them inside. "These early-blooming sunflowers are meant to be quite a sight!"

As they went into the Visitors' Centre,

a woman wearing a green T-shirt embroidered with bright yellow sunflowers stepped forward to greet them. "Welcome to Leafley!" she said cheerfully. "My name's Laura." She handed Rachel and Kirsty a large badge each, and the girls were delighted to see that they were in the shape of a sunflower with glittering golden petals and dark-brown, velvety centres. Quickly they pinned them on.

"You've come to visit us on a very special day," Laura went on. "The judges of the Best Kept Village Award are coming to Leafley today, and we're hoping we might win first prize!"

"Has Leafley ever won an award before?" asked Kirsty.

"Never," Laura replied. "So everyone's very excited and we've even planted some extra sunflowers to impress the judges!"

"Well, you must have a good chance of winning," said Mr Tate with a smile. "I've heard that the Leafley sunflowers are spectacular."

Laura's face fell. "Unfortunately most of the sunflowers haven't bloomed as early as they usually do," she sighed. "There are only a few small ones out at the moment. It's a real shame, but there's nothing we can do about it. We're hoping that the judges will think Leafley is lovely, anyway."

Rachel and Kirsty glanced at each other. They knew exactly why the Leafley sunflowers weren't blooming. Both girls silently hoped that they would find Charlotte the Sunflower Fairy's magic petal as soon as possible.

"Is that a map of the village?" Kirsty asked curiously, pointing at the wall behind Laura.

"Yes, it shows the Sunflower Trail," Laura explained. "If you follow the glittery sunflower stickers on the map, you'll get to see all the best sights in the village. The trail starts here at the Visitors' Centre, and ends here too."

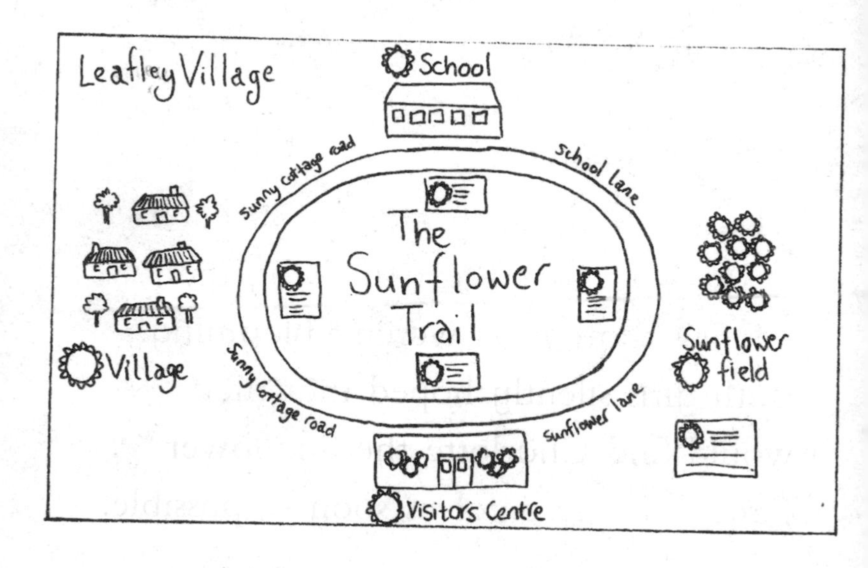

"Oh, Mum, please can Rachel and I follow the Sunflower Trail?" asked Kirsty eagerly.

"Yes, of course," Mrs Tate agreed.

"We thought we'd have a cup of tea before we go and look at Leafley ourselves," said Mr Walker, pointing to the café at the back of the Visitors' Centre. "So why don't you girls meet us back here in half an hour? Buttons can come with us," he added, taking the dog's lead from Rachel.

"You'll need this, girls," Laura handed Rachel a yellow envelope, sealed with a sparkly sunflower sticker. "It's a copy of the Sunflower Trail map for you to follow."

"Thank you," Kirsty and Rachel chorused.

The girls hurried outside, taking the envelope with them.

"Look, this is the beginning of the trail," said Kirsty, spotting a sign next to the Visitors' Centre. A golden arrow pointed the way down the lane, and there was a large, glittering sunflower with a smiley face painted next to it.

"And there's the village," added Rachel.

As the girls set off along the trail, they could see the first few houses ahead of them. They had neat front gardens planted with sunflowers, but hardly any of them were in bloom, and those that were flowering looked rather wilted and unhappy, their heads drooping and their leaves dying.

"We must find Charlotte's magic Sunflower Petal!" Rachel declared. "Maybe then Leafley will have a chance to win the Best Kept Village Award."

As she spoke, Rachel pulled the sticker off the back of the envelope that Laura had given them. Immediately a stream of dazzling golden sparkles burst out and swirled up into the air in a glistening cloud.

"Oh!" Rachel gasped.

"It looks like fairy dust!" Kirsty exclaimed. "Quick, Rachel, see what's inside!"

Carefully, Rachel pulled the envelope open, and immediately Charlotte the Sunflower Fairy danced out, waving her wand and smiling happily at the girls!

The little fairy hovered in the air, shaking out her crumpled wings and straightening her blue trousers and matching top. She had dark hair tied in bouncy bunches, and around her waist was a wide leather belt, fastened with a big, shiny sunflower buckle.

"Hello, girls!" Charlotte cried.

"I'm so glad to see you."

"We thought we might find you here, Charlotte," said Kirsty. "Is there any sign of your Sunflower Petal yet?"

Charlotte's face fell and her wings drooped. "Not yet," she said sadly. "But I know it's in Leafley somewhere. We must find it, girls!"

"We can look for your petal by following the Sunflower Trail," Rachel promised, showing Charlotte the map.

"But don't forget the goblins have a wand full of Jack Frost's icy magic to help them," Charlotte warned. "We must be careful."

Rachel was studying the map as they walked along. "This street is called Sunny Cottage Row," she announced.

There was a small group of children already on the trail ahead of them so Charlotte hid herself behind Kirsty's sunflower badge. Then the girls walked towards the row of tiny cottages. The black and white beamed houses were very pretty with their thatched roofs and colourful gardens of spring flowers. But, as the girls had already noticed, hardly any of the sunflowers were in bloom.

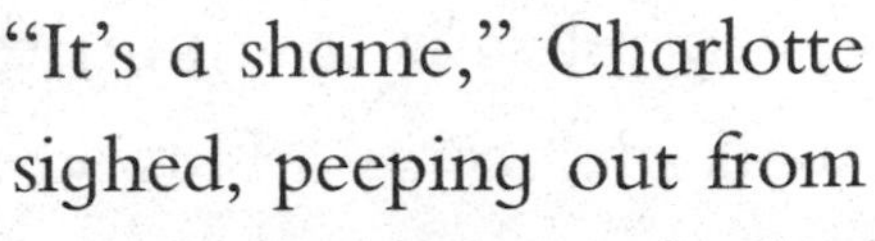

"It's a shame," Charlotte sighed, peeping out from behind Kirsty's badge as the group ahead of them moved on to the next stage of the trail. "Sunny Cottage Row is so beautiful when all the gorgeous sunflowers are out."

As they passed another pretty garden, Kirsty noticed that this one seemed to have a few more sunflowers in bloom than the others they'd seen so far. She stopped and scanned the garden carefully, searching for Charlotte's petal, but a sudden movement made her jump. Was she imagining things or had that sunflower actually twitched?

She watched it carefully for a moment,

then nudged Rachel. "One of those sunflowers is moving around!" she told her friend.

"First it was by the fence, but now it's over there by the shed!"

"Are you sure?" asked Rachel.

"Which sunflower was it, Kirsty?" Charlotte wanted to know.

Kirsty pointed it out.

"It's not moving now," Rachel remarked. Then she gave a gasp. "But that one is! Look, over by the pond!"

Rachel, Kirsty and Charlotte watched in amazement as the other sunflower ran across the garden, petals bobbing, and stopped near the shed too.

"That doesn't look like one of my beautiful sunflowers," Charlotte said doubtfully.

Rachel frowned, peering over the fence at the flower which had moved. "No, sunflowers don't have long, pointy green noses," she agreed. "That's a goblin!"

Kirsty and Charlotte looked dismayed. Now that Rachel had pointed it out, they could see that the goblin was wearing a head-dress of yellow sunflower petals which fitted neatly around his face.

"Girls, it's even worse than that!" Charlotte announced solemnly, staring

into the garden at all the sunflowers in turn. "There are lots of goblins!"

She pointed her wand at five more sunflowers in turn, including the one Kirsty had noticed. The girls' hearts sank as they realised that Charlotte was right. They were all goblins!

"So that's why I thought there were more sunflowers blooming in this garden than any of the others," Kirsty

groaned. "They're goblins in disguise!"

"If they hadn't moved, we wouldn't have noticed," Rachel said. "They blend in so well with their green bodies and their yellow head-dresses!"

"We must find out if the goblins have my magic petal," Charlotte said urgently, flying out from behind Kirsty's badge. "Girls, I'm going to turn you into fairies right away."

Rachel put the map down, and she and Kirsty stood still and waited for Charlotte to shower them with magic fairy dust. One wave of Charlotte's wand, and the girls begin to shrink. Soon they had pretty, translucent fairy wings on their backs!

Quickly Charlotte, Rachel and Kirsty zoomed into the garden where the goblins were hiding. Charlotte led the girls behind a large bush and put a finger to her lips. Then they all peeped out between the leaves.

"There's nobody on the trail now," called one of the goblins. "Quick!" He beckoned to the others, losing a couple of petals from his head-dress as he darted across the garden. "Start looking for the magic petal!"

The goblins immediately began a frantic search. They dashed all over the garden, grabbing the sunflowers roughly and pulling their heads down to examine the petals.

"Oh, I can't bear it!" Charlotte gasped, covering her eyes with her hands. "They're spoiling my poor sunflowers."

Rachel and Kirsty watched anxiously as the goblins stomped through the middle of the flower borders. *Maybe Charlotte's magic petal isn't in this garden at all,* Rachel thought doubtfully. There weren't many sunflowers left that the goblins hadn't already examined.

Except for a clump of three not far from the bush where Charlotte and the girls were hiding…

Rachel glanced at the three sunflowers. One was much taller than the others and its sunshine-yellow petals had unfurled to display the dark brown seeds in its centre. *It was very strange,* Rachel thought with a frown, *but one of the petals seemed more golden and sparkly than the others…*

"Oh!" Rachel gasped, then clapped her hand over her mouth to stop herself from crying out too loudly. "It's the magic petal!" she whispered to her friends.

"Where?" Charlotte demanded excitedly.

Rachel pointed out the tall sunflower, and Charlotte's face broke into a big, beaming smile.

"Well done, Rachel," she whispered, doing a little dance of joy in the air. "We'd better get hold of it quickly before the goblins do."

Quickly Charlotte whizzed out from behind the bush, her thin, gauzy wings a blur as she raced towards her precious petal. Rachel and Kirsty followed.

"Oh, no, you don't!" yelled a gruff voice from behind them. "That magic petal belongs to Jack Frost!"

Kirsty glanced back over her shoulder to see a goblin bearing down on the sunflower. "One of the goblins has spotted us and the magic petal!" she cried.

"Hurry, girls!" Charlotte called, her wings beating faster than ever.

Rachel and Kirsty had never flown quite so fast before as they dashed after Charlotte.

"I think we're going to get to the petal first," Kirsty panted. "The goblin's not big enough to reach it."

But just as Charlotte and the girls arrived at the sunflower, the goblin skidded to a halt on the ground below

them. He grabbed the sunflower's stem and yanked thc big flower head down towards him and away from Charlotte and the girls.

The next moment he screeched with triumph as he snatched the magic petal and waved it gleefully in the air. Charlotte, Rachel and Kirsty looked at each other in horror.

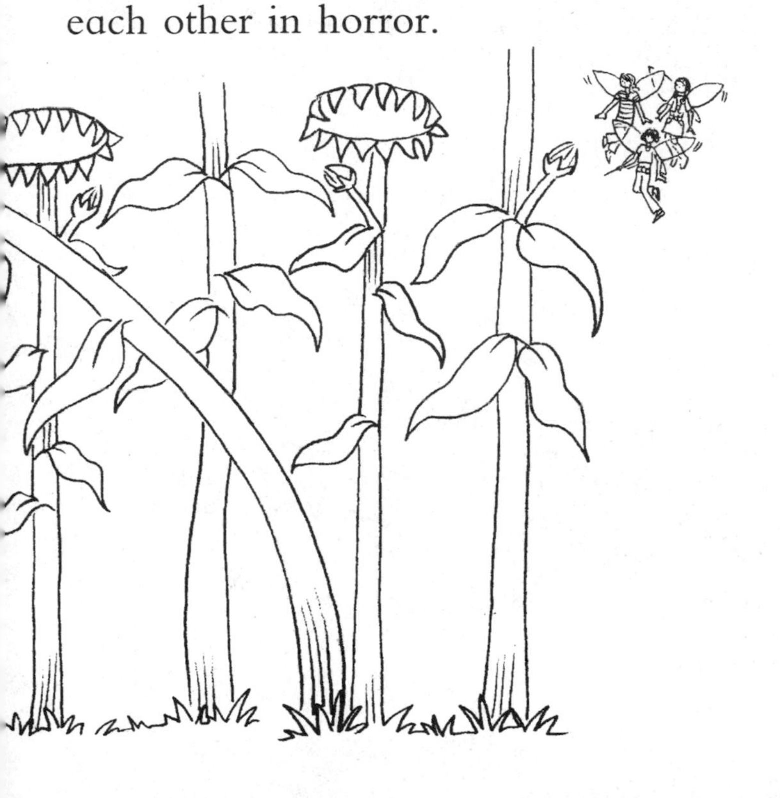

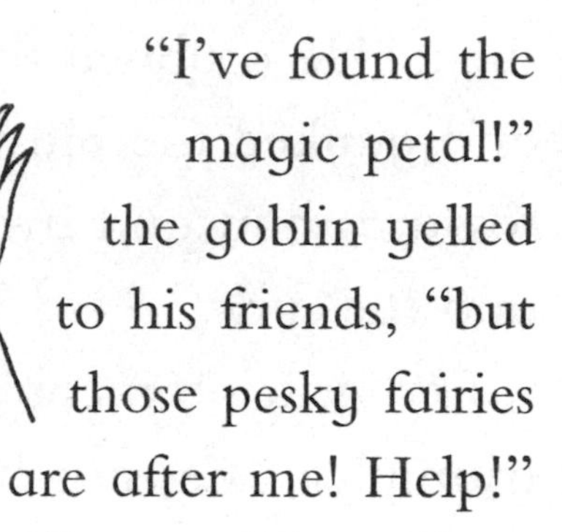

"I've found the magic petal!" the goblin yelled to his friends, "but those pesky fairies are after me! Help!"

"Don't let them get the petal!" another goblin shouted across the garden. "I'll cast a spell to get rid of them."

"That goblin's got the magic wand!" cried Kirsty.

The goblin had indeed produced the icy wand Jack Frost had given the goblins, and he was pointing it right in the direction of Charlotte, Rachel and Kirsty.

"Jack Frost's freezing icy bolts, will give those fairies a nasty shock!" he roared loudly.

Nothing happened.

"That's a terrible spell!" one of the other goblins yelled. "It doesn't work because it doesn't even rhyme!"

The goblin with the wand looked furious.

"Jack Frost's freezing icy bolts, will give those fairies nasty jolts!" he shouted triumphantly. "That rhymes!"

And this time the spell worked. Three sparkling ice bolts shot out from the wand and headed straight towards Charlotte and the girls.

"Look out!" yelled Charlotte, turning a somersault in the air as the ice bolt whizzed underneath her.

Kirsty managed to flutter aside and avoid the second ice bolt, but Rachel wasn't so lucky. The third bolt hit her and instantly surrounded her in a sheet of ice. Rachel hovered in the air for a second, her face frozen in an expression of surprise.

But then she began to tumble towards the ground, her wings frozen stiff.

"Oh, no!" Kirsty cried anxiously as the goblins cackled with glee and headed out of the garden. "If Rachel falls to the ground, she'll shatter into icy pieces!"

With a flick of her wrist, Charlotte cast a fairy spell. Glittering sparkles rained down from her wand onto the tall sunflower, surrounding it with magic.

As Rachel plummeted downwards, the sunflower bent its golden head. It caught Rachel safely, just as she was about to hit the ground, and scooped her up.

Kirsty and Charlotte zoomed over to check that Rachel wasn't hurt. She was sitting in the middle of the sunflower on a cushion of seeds, and she had the same surprised look on her face.

"She's still frozen," Kirsty said anxiously, feeling Rachel's arm. "It's like touching an icicle!"

"The goblins' spells aren't as powerful as Jack Frost's magic," explained Charlotte. "The spell should wear off soon."

Kirsty took off her cardigan and wrapped it around her friend. Then she and Charlotte watched as, very gradually, Rachel began to warm up. After a few minutes she was able to move her face, then her arms, then her legs. And soon she was fluttering her wings and looking much happier.

"Oh, I feel much better now," Rachel declared, still shivering a little. "I'm so glad I'm not a fairy popsicle anymore!

Now, where have those goblins gone with the magic petal?"

"They went further along the trail," said Kirsty, "but they can't have got very far."

As soon as Charlotte's magic had whisked the girls back up to their normal size, Rachel grabbed the map and they all hurried off along the Sunflower Trail, searching for the goblins.

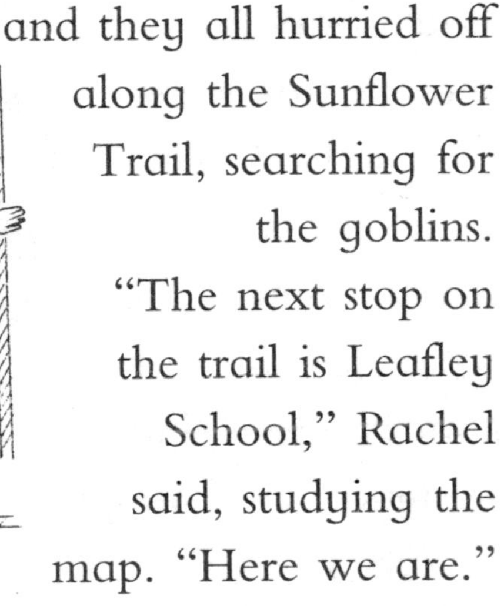

"The next stop on the trail is Leafley School," Rachel said, studying the map. "Here we are."

The girls paused outside the school to look around.

"Look at the beautiful display," said Kirsty, pointing at a huge 3-D collage which filled one entire wall of the building. The collage was of sunflowers made of yellow papier-mâché and bright green cardboard leaves. The paper petals had been sprinkled here and there with golden glitter which made them sparkle in the sun as though they were full of fairy magic.

Rachel and Charlotte gazed at the collage in delight.

"The school's closed for the Easter holidays," said Rachel, checking that the gates were locked. "So the goblins can't be hiding in there."

They moved on along the trail, but there was still no sign of the goblins.

"We're coming up to the Sunflower Field on our left," Rachel said, studying the map carefully.

"Oh, yes," sighed Charlotte, "The Sunflower Field is beautiful

when the sunflowers are blooming, but I suppose hardly any of them will be at the moment because my petal is missing." As the girls turned the corner of the trail, Kirsty saw a large field packed with tall, nodding sunflowers. She was expecting them all to be wilting like the others they'd seen. But to her surprise, right in the centre of the field, was a large circle of sunflowers in full bloom, turning their golden heads cheerfully towards the sun.

"Aren't they gorgeous?" Kirsty gasped. "They're the most beautiful sunflowers we've seen all day!" Then she frowned, because the sunflowers which had looked so beautiful just a moment ago were now beginning to droop before her very eyes!

"Ooh, look over there by the fence!" Rachel exclaimed. "There's a big patch of them, all in bloom— Oh!"

Now Rachel could hardly believe her eyes. The sunflowers she'd been staring at now looked as if they were dying as well!

"Over there, girls!" Charlotte cried, pointing her wand at the far end of the field. "Those sunflowers are lovely."

"No, they're wilting too," Rachel replied as the sunflowers Charlotte was indicating began to droop.

Charlotte looked puzzled. Then she twirled excitedly up into the air. "Girls, the goblins are here with the magic petal!" she announced. "They must be hiding in the field and my petal is making the sunflowers bloom wherever they run!"

"There go the goblins!" Rachel called, pointing at another clump of blossoming sunflowers.

Kirsty burst out laughing. "The silly goblins are running around in circles!" she pointed out.

Charlotte, Rachel and Kirsty stood and watched for a few moments as the goblins circled and zigzagged their way wildly across the field of sunflowers. They didn't seem to have any idea where they were going.

"They could be stuck in there for

hours!" Charlotte said. "How are we going to get my petal back?"

Rachel turned to Kirsty and Charlotte, beaming all over. "I think I've got an idea!" she declared.

Perfect Petals

Rachel gave the map to Kirsty and turned to the tiny fairy. "Charlotte, could you magic up two glittery paper petals like the ones on the Leafley School collage?" she asked.

Charlotte laughed. "Of course I can!" she exclaimed. "Watch!"

She twirled her wand and a shower

of magic fairy dust fell softly over Rachel. A second later two large sunflower petals appeared, one in each of Rachel's hands.

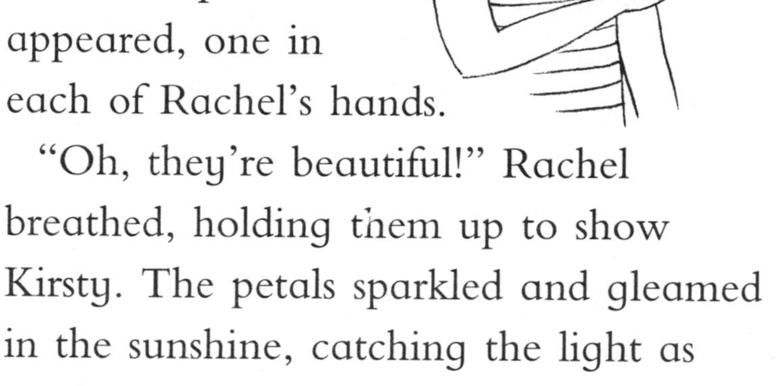

"Oh, they're beautiful!" Rachel breathed, holding them up to show Kirsty. The petals sparkled and gleamed in the sunshine, catching the light as Rachel turned them this way and that.

The goblins were still rushing around the field, clearly trying to find their way out, and making the sunflowers bloom and wilt as they went. Charlotte and the girls could hear rustling noises as the goblins pushed their way through the flower stems.

"Here goes," Rachel whispered. "Hello, goblins!" she called loudly, putting her hands behind her back. "I've got a deal for you!"

No goblins appeared, but the rustling noise suddenly stopped.

"They're listening," Kirsty whispered.

"I've got two petals," Rachel went on, keeping the petals out of sight. "And I want to swap them for your one petal!"

At that moment a green face poked out from between the sunflower stems near the fence. A goblin was scowling at the girls suspiciously.

"We're not giving you our magic petal!" he snapped.

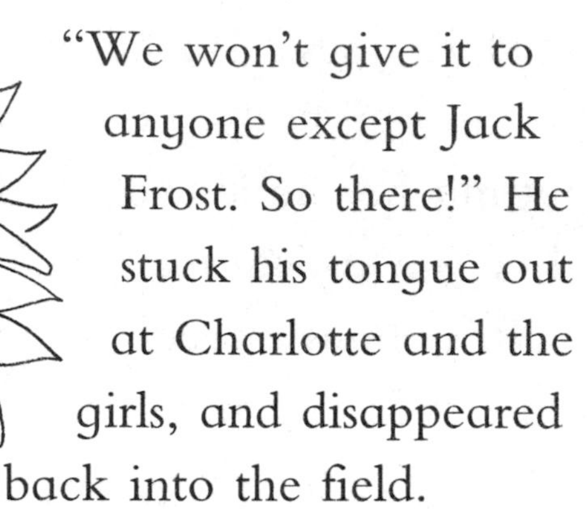

"We won't give it to anyone except Jack Frost. So there!" He stuck his tongue out at Charlotte and the girls, and disappeared back into the field.

"Don't you even want to see my petals?" asked Rachel.

A different goblin poked his head out. "Let me see!" he demanded.

Rachel held up the two petals Charlotte had given her. They looked dazzlingly beautiful in the midday sun.

"Oooh!" the goblin gasped, his eyes lighting up greedily.

"They're much bigger than your petal, aren't they?" Rachel pointed out.

"And more sparkly!" Kirsty added.

"Hey, you!" roared the first goblin crossly, sticking his head out again and glaring at the other one. "Don't talk to them!"

"But their petals are more sparkly," the second goblin said. "That must mean they're more magical!"

The first goblin stared hard at the petals in Rachel's hands. "Wait there!" he snapped at Rachel.

The two goblins disappeared again, and Charlotte and the girls could hear lots of whispering among the sunflowers. Rachel tried to look cool and calm although her heart was racing. Would the goblins accept the deal?

At last the first goblin poked his head out. "We'll trade," he announced. "But only one of you must come forward with the petals. And one of us will bring our petal to you."

Rachel nodded. Immediately one cautious-looking goblin pushed his way out of the sunflowers and came towards her. He had Charlotte's magic petal gripped tightly in his knobbly green hand.

Rachel went to meet him.

"Give me one of your petals first!" the goblin demanded rudely.

Rachel held out one sparkly petal, and the goblin snatched it quickly.

Kirsty held her breath as the goblin then held out his own petal towards Rachel.

The instant Rachel took it, he grabbed the other paper petal from her and danced gleefully back to his friends.

"I've got the two sparkly petals!" he boasted triumphantly.

There was a muffled cheer from inside the field and then Charlotte and the girls heard the sound of the goblins running off.

"The silly goblins have swapped the magic petal for two which aren't magic at all!" Kirsty chuckled.

"Yes," Charlotte laughed, whizzing over to Rachel. "I'd better take my magic petal straight back to Fairyland before the goblins realise their mistake!"

Charlotte flew down and gently tapped the petal sitting on Rachel's palm with her wand. Immediately it shrank down to its Fairyland size.

"Thank you a thousand times, girls," Charlotte cried, picking up the tiny petal and holding it lovingly. "Enjoy the rest of your visit to Leafley, and

good luck with finding the other missing petals!"

"Goodbye, Charlotte," called Kirsty and Rachel as the little fairy vanished in a burst of golden fairy magic.

"We did it, Kirsty!" Rachel beamed at her friend. "We found another magic petal!"

Kirsty glanced at her watch. "And we've still got some time before we meet our parents," she pointed out. "Shall we keep on following the Sunflower Trail?"

Rachel took out the map and unfolded it.

"That's funny." She frowned. "I don't remember seeing that before!"

Kirsty looked too and saw a small, sparkling sunflower on the map, marking the place on the path next to the field where the girls were standing.

"Is it fairy magic?" Kirsty asked, looking thrilled.

"I think Charlotte's sunflower magic must be starting to work, now that she has her petal back," Rachel said with a grin. "Look!" She pointed at the field. All the sunflowers were now standing tall and proud, turning their faces to the sun, their golden petals beginning to open.

"Rachel, look at the map!" gasped Kirsty.

The small, sparkling sunflower on the map had begun to grow a long green stem. It curled and twisted across the paper, following the path of the Sunflower Trail. As Kirsty and Rachel

hurried along the trail, following the stem, they noticed with delight that sunflowers were bursting into bloom all around them. It was a wonderful sight.

"All the gardens look beautiful!" Rachel said happily. "And even the sunflower decorations look as if they've just been freshly painted!"

"I think every sunflower in Leafley is in bloom," Kirsty laughed.

As the girls reached the Visitors' Centre, they saw a group of men and women coming out carrying clipboards and maps of the Sunflower Trail.

"Do you think they're the judges for the Best Kept Village award?" Rachel whispered to Kirsty.

Kirsty nodded. "It looks like Charlotte's sunflower magic has come to the rescue just in time!" she whispered back.

As the girls went inside the Visitors' Centre, they couldn't help overhearing two of the judges talking.

"I know we've seen some beautiful villages while we've been judging this

competition," said one of the women. "But those gardens in Sunny Cottage Row over there look absolutely spectacular! The sunflowers are beautiful."

"I know," the other judge replied. "I can't wait to see the sunflowers around the rest of the trail." She lowered her voice. "Between you and me, I think we may be looking at our winning village!"

Kirsty and Rachel stared at each other in delight.

"Isn't Petal Magic brilliant?" Rachel whispered. Kirsty nodded happily.

The Petal Fairies

Charlotte the Sunflower Fairy has got her magic petal back. Now Rachel and Kirsty must help

Olivia the Orchid Fairy

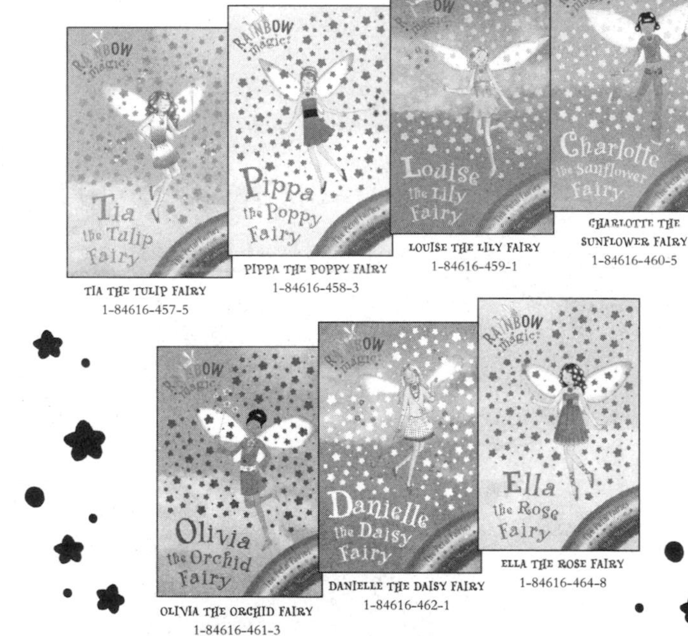

TIA THE TULIP FAIRY
1-84616-457-5

PIPPA THE POPPY FAIRY
1-84616-458-3

LOUISE THE LILY FAIRY
1-84616-459-1

CHARLOTTE THE SUNFLOWER FAIRY
1-84616-460-5

OLIVIA THE ORCHID FAIRY
1-84616-461-3

DANIELLE THE DAISY FAIRY
1-84616-462-1

ELLA THE ROSE FAIRY
1-84616-464-8

Win Rainbow Magic goodies!

In every book in the Rainbow Magic Petal Fairies series (books 43-49) there is a hidden picture of a petal with a secret letter in it. Find all seven letters and re-arrange them to make a special Petal Fairies word, then send it to us. Each month we will put the entries into a draw and select one winner to receive a Rainbow Magic Sparkly T-shirt and Goody Bag!

Send your entry on a postcard to Rainbow Magic Fun Day Competition, Orchard Books, 338 Euston Road, London NW1 3BH. Australian readers should write to Hachette Children's Books, Level 17/207 Kent Street, Sydney, NSW 2000. New Zealand readers should write to Rainbow Magic Competition, 4 Whetu Place, Mairangi Bay, Auckland, NZ. Don't forget to include your name and address. Only one entry per child. Final draw: 30th April 2008.

Good luck!

by Daisy Meadows

The Rainbow Fairies

Ruby the Red Fairy	ISBN	978 1 84362 016 7
Amber the Orange Fairy	ISBN	978 1 84362 017 4
Saffron the Yellow Fairy	ISBN	978 1 84362 018 1
Fern the Green Fairy	ISBN	978 1 84362 019 8
Sky the Blue Fairy	ISBN	978 1 84362 020 4
Izzy the Indigo Fairy	ISBN	978 1 84362 021 1
Heather the Violet Fairy	ISBN	978 1 84362 022 8

The Weather Fairies

Crystal the Snow Fairy	ISBN	978 1 84362 633 6
Abigail the Breeze Fairy	ISBN	978 1 84362 634 3
Pearl the Cloud Fairy	ISBN	978 1 84362 635 0
Goldie the Sunshine Fairy	ISBN	978 1 84362 636 7
Evie the Mist Fairy	ISBN	978 1 84362 637 4
Storm the Lightning Fairy	ISBN	978 1 84362 638 1
Hayley the Rain Fairy	ISBN	978 1 84362 641 1

The Party Fairies

Cherry the Cake Fairy	ISBN	978 1 84362 818 7
Melodie the Music Fairy	ISBN	978 1 84362 819 4
Grace the Glitter Fairy	ISBN	978 1 84362 820 0
Honey the Sweet Fairy	ISBN	978 1 84362 821 7
Polly the Party Fun Fairy	ISBN	978 184362 822 4
Phoebe the Fashion Fairy	ISBN	978 1 84362 823 1
Jasmine the Present Fairy	ISBN	978 1 84362 824 8

The Jewel Fairies

India the Moonstone Fairy	ISBN	978 1 84362 958 0
Scarlett the Garnet Fairy	ISBN	978 1 84362 954 2
Emily the Emerald Fairy	ISBN	978 1 84362 955 9
Chloe the Topaz Fairy	ISBN	978 1 84362 956 6
Amy the Amethyst Fairy	ISBN	978 1 84362 957 3
Sophie the Sapphire Fairy	ISBN	978 1 84362 953 5
Lucy the Diamond Fairy	ISBN	978 1 84362 959 7

The Pet Keeper Fairies

Katie the Kitten Fairy	ISBN	978 1 84616 166 7
Bella the Bunny Fairy	ISBN	978 1 84616 170 4
Georgia the Guinea Pig Fairy	ISBN	978 1 84616 168 1
Lauren the Puppy Fairy	ISBN	978 1 84616 169 8
Harriet the Hamster Fairy	ISBN	978 1 84616 167 4
Molly the Goldfish Fairy	ISBN	978 1 84616 172 8
Penny the Pony Fairy	ISBN	978 1 84616 171 1

The Fun Day Fairies

Megan the Monday Fairy	ISBN	978 184616 188 9
Tallulah the Tuesday Fairy	ISBN	978 1 84616 189 6
Willow the Wednesday Fairy	ISBN	978 1 84616 190 2
Thea the Thursday Fairy	ISBN	978 1 84616 191 9
Freya the Friday Fairy	ISBN	978 1 84616 192 6
Sienna the Saturday Fairy	ISBN	978 1 84616 193 3
Sarah the Sunday Fairy	ISBN	978 1 84616 194 0

Holly the Christmas Fairy	ISBN	978 1 84362 661 9
Summer the Holiday Fairy	ISBN	978 1 84362 960 3
Stella the Star Fairy	ISBN	978 1 84362 869 9
Kylie the Carnival Fairy	ISBN	978 1 84616 175 9
Paige the Pantomime Fairy	ISBN	978 1 84616 047 9
The Rainbow Magic Treasury	ISBN	978 1 84616 209 1

Coming soon:

Flora the Fancy Dress Fairy	ISBN	978 1 84616 505 4

All priced at £3.99. *Holly the Christmas Fairy, Summer the Holiday Fairy, Stella the Star Fairy, Kylie the Carnival Fairy, Paige the Pantomime Fairy and Flora the Fancy Dress Fairy* are priced at £5.99. *The Rainbow Magic Treasury* is priced at £12.99.
Rainbow Magic books are available from all good bookshops, or can be ordered direct from the publisher: Orchard Books, PO BOX 29, Douglas IM99 1BQ
Credit card orders please telephone 01624 836000
or fax 01624 837033 or visit our Internet site: www.wattspub.co.uk
or e-mail: bookshop@enterprise.net for details.

To order please quote title, author and ISBN and your full name and address.
Cheques and postal orders should be made payable to 'Bookpost plc.'
Postage and packing is FREE within the UK
(overseas customers should add £2.00 per book).
Prices and availability are subject to change.

Look out for the Dance Fairies!

BETHANY
THE BALLET FAIRY
978-1-84616-490-3

JADE
THE DISCO FAIRY
978-1-84616-491-0

REBECCA
THE ROCK 'N' ROLL FAIRY
978-1-84616-492-7

TASHA
THE TAP DANCE FAIR
978-1-84616-493-4

JESSICA
THE JAZZ FAIRY
978-1-84616-495-8

SASKIA
THE SALSA FAIRY
978-1-84616-496-5

IMOGEN
THE ICE DANCE FAIRY
978-1-84616-497-2

Available Now!